BAKUGAN
BATTLE BRAWLERS

P9-EGN-739

THE BATTLE BRAWLERS

BY TRACY WEST

SCHOLASTIC INC.

NEW YORK   TORONTO   LONDON   AUCKLAND   SYDNEY

MEXICO CITY   NEW DELHI   HONG KONG   BUENOS AIRES

ISBN-13: 978-0-545-11751-7
ISBN-10: 0-545-11751-8

© SPIN MASTER LTD/SEGA TOYS.

12 11 10 9 8 7 6 5   9 10 11 12 13 14/0

INTERIOR DESIGNED BY HENRY NG
PRINTED IN THE U.S.A
FIRST PRINTING, JANUARY 2009

CHAPTER 1

TIME FOR A BRAWL!

an Kuso raced home from school. He ran into his house and slammed the front door behind him.

"Hey mom! I'm home!" Daniel shouted as he ran up to his room.

His mom sat on the living room floor, twisted up like a pretzel. A yoga DVD played on the TV.

"Daniel! I put your lunch in the refrigerator. And please don't forget to wash up!" she called upstairs.

"Thanks, Mom!" Daniel called back.

Daniel threw his backpack on his bed and opened the top drawer of his dresser. Inside was a small, white box. He opened the lid and smiled.

"Okay, time to check out my stash!"

The box was filled with small red-and-gold balls. Each one was about the size of a large walnut.

"Hmm, let's see. I'll take this," he said, picking up

one of the balls. "Oh, my Saurus! And this one for sure. All set!"

Dan stuffed the three balls into his pocket and charged downstairs.

"Daniel, your lunch is getting cold," his mom said as he ran past.

"Then why'd you put it in the fridge?" Dan joked.

"Don't get smart with me, young man!" his mom scolded.

Daniel hurried outside. Lunch would just have to wait.

It was time for a Bakugan Brawl!

Dan's brown hair blew behind him as he zoomed down the street. He was dressed in the same colors as his Bakugan — red pants, gold T-shirt, and red vest.

Sometimes Dan still couldn't believe that Bakugan was real. Life was normal, and then all of a sudden, everything had changed. Cards had started dropping down from the sky like rain. At first, nobody knew where they were from or who had sent them. But then kids all over the world started playing with the cards — and invented a wicked new game called Bakugan.

That's when the power of the cards was revealed. Each one held its own battling beast that came to life when you threw it down. The battles were intense. Kids created Bakugan websites to share battle stats and get tips. Dan had made a lot of new friends thanks to Bakugan.

But the Bakugan brawler waiting for him in the park was no friend. Akira was an annoying kid from school. He had challenged Dan to a battle, and Dan was just itching to beat him.

Akira was waiting by a park bench. He was short, with an overbite and freckles sprinkled across his nose. He wore a green shirt and a backwards baseball cap on his head. And he wasn't alone. There was someone sitting on the park bench behind Akira — a really *big* someone.

"Sorry I'm late!" Dan said, jumping off of his bike.

Akira snickered. "And here I thought ya might have chickened out."

"Doubt that, Akira," Dan shot back. "And who'd you bring with you? Hope it's backup, 'cause you'll need it!"

Akira grinned. "Your battle isn't with me, Danny boy."

The person on the bench stood up. It was a kid — a very tall, very wide, kid.

"Whoa!" Dan said. He had been set up! "Hey, I don't think this is very fair."

"My little bro here says you think you're pretty good," said the large kid. "Well I guess it's time to find out how good you really are!"

"Yeah, I'm pretty good," Dan said confidently. "What about you? What's your deal?"

"My name is Shuji, and I'm master of Subterra Space!" Shuji boasted.

Dan was shocked. He knew the Bakugan beasts were divided up into six worlds, and then divided up into classes. But Bakugan was so new that he didn't know all of the worlds and classes yet.

"You've got to be joking. I've never heard of Subterra before!" he cried. He shook his head. "Great. How am I supposed to battle against a beast that doesn't even exist?"

"Quit your stallin'!" Shuji yelled angrily.

Dan took a deep breath. He started forming a plan. "Okay. Let's do this. But I gotta warn you, I've never lost a battle before."

"Let's go!" Akira urged.

The park was shaped like a circle with trees all around it. Dan and Shuji stood across from each other on the circle. Then they each held up a Gate Card. The faces of the cards were black, printed with the six Bakugan world symbols.

"Bakugan, Field Open!" they both yelled.

They held up their cards, and all time and space outside the circle froze. The birds in the park stopped in mid-flight. Everything would stand still until the battle was over.

"Gate Card Set!" the boys yelled next. They each threw their cards to the opposite ends of the circle.

As the cards flew through the air, the colorful world

symbols began to glow. They whirled and twirled in the air, freezing space and time around them. The cards landed in the circle, end to end, creating a big rectangle-shaped battlefield in front of Dan and Shuji. The stage for the brawl was set.

"Ready or not, here I come!" Shuji yelled. He held up a brown and yellow Bakugan ball. Then he tossed it out onto the field.

The ball rolled and landed on the card Shuji had thrown out.

"Bakugan Stand!"

The ball stopped, and the Bakugan beast emerged from the ball. It slowly took shape, growing larger every second.

"Whoa! Freaky!" Dan cried. The beast looked like a praying mantis, with bulging yellow eyes and a mouthful of razor-sharp teeth. The giant bug stomped a hairy foot on the ground in front of Dan. He jumped back and quickly flipped open the Baku-pod he wore on his wrist.

"Welcome, Dan," the computer said. "Opponent: Subterra Mantris. Power Level 270 Gs. No other data available."

"Oh, great," Dan said, worried. 270 Gs was a decent amount of power. In a Bakugan brawl, the beast with the most points won a battle. "Okay, 'terra' means earth and his power level's at 270, so at least I know what kind of beast I'm dealing with. Question is, what should I counter with?"

It didn't take long to choose. He grinned and tossed one of his red and gold balls out onto the field. The ball landed on the same card as Shuji's Mantris.

"Your little bug is going down!" Dan boasted. "Bakugan Stand!"

The ball opened up, revealing the beast inside: a huge snake with a gold pattern across its giant red body. Deadly fangs protruded from its mouth.

"Power level 320 Gs," the Baku-pod announced.

Dan and Shuji stared at each other. Their Bakugan were standing on the same card.

"Bakugan Brawl!" the boys shouted at once.

CHAPTER 2

BURNED BY FRAME FIRE!

an was confident. His Bakugan had more G power. His Serpenoid lunged at Mantris and wrapped its powerful body around the big bug.

"All right!" Dan cheered.

But Shuji smiled smugly. "Gate Card open up now!" he yelled.

The card flipped over, revealing the holo sector. The field changed to a sandy plain with pyramids in the distance. Dan groaned as he saw that the card gave a +150 power boost to all Subterran monsters.

"Power Level Increase to 420 Gs," confirmed the Baku-pod.

Now Mantris had more power than Serpenoid. The Mantris leaped out of the snake's grasp and slashed at Serpenoid with its sharp arms. Serpenoid rolled back into its Bakugan ball.

"Not good," Dan said, as he watched his ball roll off of the field.

"You're toast!" Shuji cried out. His Bakugan turned back into a ball and bounced into his hand. Shuji got Dan's Gate Card back, too, for winning the battle.

"Battle One terminated. Subterra Mantris . . . victorious," reported the Baku-pod.

Shuji laughed. "Oh man, that was easy! You fell faster than a deck of cards in a tornado!"

Dan didn't let Shuji get to him. A Bakugan battle wasn't over until all of one player's beasts had been eliminated from the game. Dan still had two Bakugan left.

Shuji held up a brown and orange ball. "Time to finish what I started!" he said. "Bakugan Stand!"

The ball landed right on the remaining Gate Card on the field. The Bakugan opened up, transforming into an enormous brown and orange creature that looked like a beetle with a sturdy body and long, sharp pincers. Two blank, blue eyes glowed from its round, flat head. A hinged jaw opened sideways to reveal a mouth full of pointy teeth.

The beast was pretty impressive. But Dan stayed cool.

"Ya think you're pretty good, huh?" he said. "Well, you better buckle up, Shuji, because you're going down!"

Dan held up another red and gold Bakugan ball. "Bakugan Brawl!"

He tossed the ball out onto the field, and his aim was perfect. His ball landed right in front of Shuji's Subterra beast.

"Bakugan Stand!" Dan yelled.

The ball opened up in a bright flash of red light. The creature was a Pyrus from the Falconeer class. It had the body of a human and the head of an eagle, and it flew above the field. Large, red wings grew from its back, and its hands and feet ended in sharp claws.

"Bakugan Gate Open!"

The Gate Card flipped over and the field became covered in a sea of raging flames. The card gave an extra G-power boost to Dan's beast. Shuji cried out as the Falconeer flew at the giant beetle, slamming into it and taking it down. The beetle turned back into a Bakugan ball and bounced in front of Shuji's feet.

"Huh?" Shuji looked shocked.

"It's all tied up!" Dan said happily.

Shuji scowled. "Not for long!" he yelled. He threw out a new card. "Gate Card Set!"

"Round Three begins," announced the Baku-pod. Dan looked down at the score. Shuji had collected 400 Holo Sector Points so far. Dan had 200 HSP. He'd need to capture Gate Cards with high HSP to catch up to Shuji. But he was ready.

Both boys threw out their Bakugan at the same time.

"Bakugan Stand!" they yelled.

The two balls landed on the Gate Card. Shuji's beast looked like a heavily-armored brown and gold rhino. A large horn grew from the tip of the rhino's nose, and four horns grew from the top of its head. It was a Subterran of the Saurus class, a type of Bakugan known for its tough brawling style.

Dan's Bakugan was a Saurus, too. But his Saurus was a Pyrus attribute, associated with the element of fire. It looked like Shuji's Saurus, except it was red and gold.

The two Saurus locked their massively muscled arms and grappled for control of the field. But Shuji's Saurus had 320 Gs — Dan's only had 200. Without a G-power boost, Dan would lose this battle.

But Dan had a card up his sleeve.

"Ability Activate! Saurus Glow!" he yelled as he threw the card onto the field.

Shuji gave a panicked yell as the Special Ability Card gave Dan's Saurus extra power. The red beast pummeled the brown beast with a powerful punch. Shuji's Saurus rolled back into a Bakugan ball.

"No, this can't be happening!" Shuji wailed.

Dan retrieved his Bakugan ball and grinned. "Hate to tell ya, bud, but it looks like you're down to your Subterra Mantris. And if I figured right, one more itsy-bitsy battle should put you away for good!"

Shuji growled angrily and threw out another card. "We'll just see about that, punk! Gate Card Open!"

Shuji threw out his Mantris. "Bakugan Brawl!"

Dan threw out his Falconeer. "Bakugan Brawl!"

"This battle is all mine!" Shuji called out. "Now to play *my* Ability Card."

He threw a card out onto the field, and the Mantris's front arms and claws began to glow. "Slice Cutter."

"Wow, I'm impressed," Dan said. "But if you think you're the only one holding an ace, you're wrong. Counter-Ability Activate! Frame Fire!"

Dan threw out a card, and a ring of flames shot up from the field, surrounding his Falconeer. A fireball formed in the creature's claw, and the Falconeer hurled it at Mantris. Shuji's Subterran curled back into its Bakugan Ball. Dan won the cards on the field — and all of their HSP. His points shot up to 1300.

"Game, set and match — Dan!" the Baku-pod announced.

Dan grinned. "It looks like I win!"

CHAPTER 3

INSIDE THE PARALLEL UNIVERSE

That night, Dan went online to tell his friends about his latest battle. Even though they all lived in different places, they could talk and see each other thanks to the webcams on their computers.

Dan had his four best friends up on-screen. In the upper left was Runo, a girl Dan's age with green eyes and blue hair that she wore in two ponytails. Next to her was Marucho, a boy with yellow hair and eyeglasses. At 11, he was a year younger and a lot shorter than the other brawlers, but he made up for that with his knowledge of Bakugan.

Alice, a girl with red hair and thoughtful brown eyes, was in the lower left corner of Dan's screen. And finally there was silver-haired Julie, who always seemed to be smiling.

Dan kicked back in his desk chair as he bragged about the battle.

"And then I let him have it with my secret weapon, Frame Fire!" Dan told his friends. "Man, you should've seen me. I was like, totally wicked! Then again, what would you expect from the greatest Bakugan Brawler?"

"Whatever," said Runo, slightly annoyed. "I just checked the world rankings and you're sitting at 121!"

"That's impossible!" Dan blurted. "I've got to check myself."

He clicked on the Bakugan website and checked the player rankings page. "Scrolling up . . . ha! I'm 117!"

Runo rolled her eyes. "Please, give me a break! You should save your breath until you break into the top ten."

"Yeah right, like you're one to talk," Dan shot back. "You're not even ranked."

He stuck out his tongue. Runo shook her head. "Like that's real mature!"

"Danny, that's so dreamy!" Julie interrupted in her bubbly voice. "One seventeen! That's up four whole spots in one day."

Marucho adjusted his eyeglasses. "Dan, may I suggest you set your sights on Shun?" he suggested, his voice nervous. "He's ranked number one and in a few years you could surpass him."

Alice frowned. "In a few years? There has to be some way you could challenge him or something, isn't there?"

"I bet I could take him," Dan replied. "I don't mean to brag, you know, but no one's ever even come close to beating me at this game."

Dan turned away from the camera. Marucho's idea was starting to sound pretty good. *Better look out, Shun, because I am gonna take you down!* he promised himself.

Far away, Shun was sitting on his front porch, staring at the glowing moon in the night sky. He was thinking about Bakugan, too.

"Defending my ranking has been a joke when battling these amateurs," he told himself. "What I need is a serious challenger. One who understands the power that lies in the Vestroia dimension . . ."

The Vestroia dimension.

Dan and his friends didn't know a lot about it. This parallel universe was where the Bakugan cards had been created. There, Bakugan beasts lived freely.

In a space filled with swirling yellow and red flames, a red Dragonoid beast watched the action on Earth with interest. The beast, Drago, had glowing green eyes, large brown wings, and a body covered with red scales.

If only the human they call Dan could understand that Bakugan is not just a game, Drago thought. *An even larger battle is taking place in my universe, Vestroia. A universe fueled by six worlds, each with its own element.*

The earth element, called Subterra.

The element of Light — Haos.

The Dark Element — Darkus.

Aquos, or what humans would call the water element.

The wind element, Ventus.

And the fire element, Pyrus.

Drago's thoughts were interrupted as a silver-gray Dragonoid burst into Pyrus space.

"Naga! Wait!" Drago cried.

The Dragonoid angrily flapped his wings. "Out of my way, Drago!"

"Why are you so obsessed with gaining all of this power, Naga?" Drago asked. "You know that it will only lead to your ultimate destruction!"

"Silence!" Naga cried. "You have no idea what we feel inside. You know nothing of our world!"

"I suspect you were the one behind the human they call Michael," Drago said. "What I'd like to know is: where did you find him?"

Naga laughed. He held up his claw, which clutched a Bakugan card. "Do you know what this is?"

Before Drago could answer, Naga tossed the card in front of him. The card grew, and colors began to swirl on the card's face.

"A portal!" Drago cried.

"Yes, and it leads to the source of the power!" Naga cried. He flew into the card, right into a tunnel of swirling light.

"But to where?" Drago asked.

"The dimension of Vestroia!" Naga cried.

Then he vanished into the portal.

CHAPTER 4

POWER SURGE!

Dan walked to school early the next morning, thinking of a strategy for beating Shun.

But Shuji had other ideas. The big bully stood on the sidewalk, blocking Dan's way. Akira stood behind him.

"I want a rematch!" Shuji demanded.

"Gimme a break. You like losing?" Dan asked.

"Just zip it!" Shuji snapped. "Either we brawl or I let my fists do the talking!"

Behind him, Akira made a fist. "Yeah!"

The threat didn't scare Dan. But he wasn't about to turn down a chance to brawl. He and Shuji each held up their first card.

"Bakugan Field Open!" they both yelled.

The two cards formed a battle field between the boys. Shuji held up a black and purple Bakugan ball.

"Let's do this. Bakugan Brawl!" he yelled, throwing out his beast.

The ball landed right in the center of the Gate Card Shuji had thrown out. A purple light began to glow from the ball.

"Bakugan Stand!" Shuji commanded.

The light exploded, and a massive beast appeared on the field. It looked like a turtle with a black and purple shell. Purple spikes stuck out from the shell. Its big mouth opened and the beast let out a loud roar.

"Oh no!" Dan cried. The beast was assigned to the planet Darkus, and Darkus beasts were well known for their powers of destruction. Dan had heard of them before, but he'd never had to battle one.

"How in the world did you get ahold of a Darkus beast?" he asked.

"Here's a thought, kid," Shuji replied. "Why don't you call me Master of Darkus?"

"Gimme a break," Dan shot back. "If I'm gonna call you anything, it's loser."

Shuji angrily stomped his feet. "I've had it with you! Are we gonna do this or what?"

"Sure. Just give me a minute, would ya?" Dan asked. He thoughtfully tossed his three Bakugan balls in one hand. "Now what should I counter with? Something big or small . . . I got it!"

He threw one of the balls out onto the field. "Bakugan Brawl!"

The ball bounced over the Gate Card with Shuji's

Darkus beast and landed on the first card, the one Dan had thrown out. He was hoping Shuji didn't have another Darkus on his team. This way, he could avoid battling the giant turtle.

"Bakugan Stand!" Dan yelled, and his ball transformed into his Pyrus Saurus.

"Ha! Come on, you've got to be kidding," Shuji sneered. "That's it! That's all you've got?"

"Hey, didn't anyone ever tell you not to jump to conclusions?" Dan replied.

"It's your funeral," Shuji shot back. "Bakugan Brawl!"

He threw out his second beast, and it landed right in front of Dan's Saurus.

"Darkus Stingslash Stand!" Shuji yelled.

The ball opened up and turned into a creature that looked like a large black and purple scorpion with a human face. Its long tail had a sharp stinger on the end.

Dan cried out in horror. It was one evil-looking beast!

"Darkus Stinglash Power Level 330 Gs," the Bakupod announced. "Saurus Power Level 280 Gs."

Stinglash lashed out at Saurus with its tail. Saurus grabbed the tail, straining to push the beast back.

"Ah, looks like I need a little power boost," Dan realized. "Bakugan Gate Card Open!"

The card flipped over to reveal the Holo Sector side.

"Saurus Power Boost to 310 Gs," said the Baku-pod.

Man, this is not looking good, Dan thought. *If I don't find a way to boost Saurus by at least twenty or more, my beast is fried!*

But Dan's turn was over — he had no more moves left. Stingslash roared, hitting Saurus with its tail. Saurus flew back, and then collapsed into its Bakugan ball.

Shuji laughed. "So how does it feel to lose good and proper, Danny?"

But Dan just smiled confidently. "Hey, this battle is far from over!"

While Dan and Shuji battled, Naga emerged from the portal in Vestroia. Violet light glowed in this new space.

"Yes, I have reached the center of the universe!" Naga said triumphantly.

The Dragonoid could see two glowing spheres in front of him: a golden yellow orb, and a larger, pale blue one that pulsated with energy.

"There they are — the two conflicting forces, Infinity and Silence," Naga said. "They keep the Vestroia dimension in Balance. If I can absorb these two energies, I can unite with Hal-G and together we can conquer Earth and Vestroia!"

Naga flew closer to the orbs, and their glowing light illuminated his body.

"The power! Feel the glorious power!"

Arcs of rainbow light shot from the orbs, piercing Naga's body.

"More! Excellent! The power! The infinite power building inside of me!" he cried.

But the power suddenly became intense, and Naga knew that things had gone wrong. The arcs of light began to pull him into the big blue orb, and Naga couldn't fight the force.

"No! What's happened? An overload of negative energy! I can't control the balance. Too much! Too much! Noooooooooooo!"

His cries grew silent as the blue orb sucked him inside. The orb swirled violently, sending strong pulses of energy throughout the six worlds of Vestroia.

In the world of Pyrus, Drago could feel the energy's pull. He flapped his wings, struggling to fight it.

Then a black and purple beast flew into Pyrus, nearly striking him.

"What is a Darkus Bakugan doing in Pyrus space?" Drago wondered. "This must be Naga's doing!"

The Darkus beast had long arms, giant claws, and a sinister face. It turned and flew straight at Drago, slamming into him. The walls of Pyrus space rippled with the impact.

Back on the battlefield, Dan and Shuji each threw out new Bakugan. Shuji used his Stingslash again, and Dan used his Pyrus Serpenoid. The two beasts faced each other on the field, ready to battle.

Then, suddenly, Dan's Serpenoid began to shoot out huge flames, and a wave of fire and flames appeared in the sky above. Shuji didn't seem to notice, but Dan stared, transfixed. Through the haze, it looked like he could see two Bakugan battling — a Pyrus Dragonoid and a strange Darkus beast.

"It's like a new dimension is filling our Bakugan with more power," Dan realized. "Right in the middle of the battlefield! Why does my Bakugan have bigger flames? I've never seen this before!"

The vision in the sky disappeared as quickly as it came. Dan shook his head.

"That was totally weird," he said.

"Enough fooling around," Shuji called out. "It's time to end this battle. Darkus Stingslash attack!"

Stingslash's tail lunged forward, ready to strike. But before it could, Serpenoid wrapped its body around the tail, stopping it. Shuji looked shocked to see his beast attacked.

"Hey, Shuji. What happened? Scared your Stingslash can't handle the pressure?" Dan shouted at him. "Command Card. Quartet Battle Activate, now!"

Dan grinned as his Gate Card flipped over, revealing a Command Card on the flip side. When a Command Card was used, each player had to do what the card demanded. This one allowed Dan to bring more beasts into the battle.

"Get ready, Shuji, 'cause a few more Bakugan have been invited to the party!" Dan warned.

But before Dan could throw more Bakugan, he noticed that his last card was glowing strangely in his hand. A white light blanked out the Holo Sector-side of the card. Now, a new card face was forming!

"My Ability Card is transforming!" Dan cried. He watched in amazement as a glowing orb of light emerged from his card. Across the field, the same thing was happening to Shuji.

Dan's orb turned into a Pyrus Bakugan ball and landed on the field. Shuji's orb turned into a Darkus ball and landed right next to it.

Dan looked down at his Ability Card. It was a Character Card now, and it showed a picture of a Pyrus beast that looked like a red, winged dragon.

"Whoa! Isn't this a Dragonoid's Card?" Dan wondered.

Things got even weirder on the field. The two balls opened up and transformed. Dan's ball turned into the Dragonoid beast on his card. Shuji's transformed into a Darkus beast.

"Whoa, those are the same beasts I saw in my vision!" Dan exclaimed.

The two beasts charged at each other and locked together in a death grip. They flew above the field.

"You must come to your senses!" Drago said.

Dan looked around the field. That wasn't Shuji's voice he had just heard.

"Who said that?" he said, looking up at the Dragonoid. "Was it you?"

"Fear Ripper! Snap out of it!" Drago told the Darkus beast. "The negative energies of the Silent Core have taken over your power of reason!"

Dan couldn't believe it. Was the Bakugan talking? "My ears aren't playing tricks on me, are they?" he wondered.

Fear Ripper's huge claws dug into Drago's wings. *His power is building!* Drago realized. He didn't want to fight Fear Ripper, but he had to defend himself.

"Boosted Dragon!" Drago cried.

He opened his mouth and a huge fireball shot out. The ball of flame engulfed Fear Ripper, taking him down. Drago had won the battle.

The Bakugan field disappeared. Shuji sat on the ground, dejected.

Akira ran up to him. "Are you okay, man?"

"I lost again!" Shuji wailed.

Dan stared at the Bakugan in his hand. "I don't get it. I thought Bakugan was just a game. There's got to be more to it. And I've got to find out what!"

That night, Dan sat on the edge of his bed. He held Drago's ball in his hand.

"Okay, if you're there, talk to me, 'cause I want to get to the bottom of this," he said.

He waited, but no sound came from the ball. Dan sighed.

"Oh man, this is totally pointless. It's just a game piece," he realized. "But I heard it. I thought I heard it talking, didn't I?"

Dan shook his head. "Oh boy, I'm losing my mind," he said. Then he smiled. "But I'm sure I heard it. And seeing as you're a Dragonoid, I'm gonna call you Drago. Sweet! That's your new name, buddy. Hope ya like it! Well, time to hook up the web. Night, Drago!"

Dan logged in to his computer. His best friends were on the screen. Marucho smiled to see him.

"Dan, you're there!" Marucho said happily.

"Hey, guys, you're not going to believe this," Dan said. "I was brawling with this dude named Shuji when I thought I heard my Bakugan talk!"

"No way! You too?" Runo asked.

Dan was confused. "What do you mean, Runo? Are you saying someone else heard them too?"

"You should log on to the Bakugan site!" Julie said. "It's what everyone's talking about, Dan!"

Dan switched over to the site. He couldn't believe what he saw. Kids everywhere were saying their Bakugan had talked to them.

That meant he hadn't been hearing things after all.

"It *did* talk!" Dan realized. "Maybe the Bakugan world has more to it than we thought."

CHAPTER 7

MASQUERADE

The next morning, Runo walked to school, holding one of her yellow and white Haos Bakugan balls.

"How annoying," she said, frustrated. "How come Dan's Bakugan ball talks and you don't?"

Runo was walking through a playground. She wore a yellow shirt, a white skirt, and maroon fingerless gloves. She stopped in front of the monkey bars and tapped on the Bakugan ball with her finger.

"Oh come on, if you're inside there, at least say something," Runo pleaded. "Pretty please with sugar?"

The ball still didn't talk. Runo decided to stop being nice.

"Say something!" she demanded.

Suddenly, a strong wind whipped through the playground. The swings on the swingset rattled back and forth. Runo turned around to see a person wearing a long, white coat standing there, his back to her.

"Where'd you come from?" Runo asked.

The person didn't answer — but held up a Gate Card instead.

"A Battle Brawler," Runo realized. "Are you challenging me to a battle? 'Cause if you are, let's get this party started!"

Runo took one of her own Gate Cards from her bag and held it up. "Didn't catch your name."

"I never said it," replied her opponent. "Call me Masquerade."

Masquerade turned his head slightly, and Runo could see that he had wavy yellow hair — and a mask over his face.

Without another word, Runo and Masquerade threw down their Gate Cards. The swings froze in mid-movement as time and space slowed down around them, and the Bakugan field formed.

Suddenly, everything went dark. A creature flew out of the blackness — a beast with red glowing eyes in its bare skull. Purple and black striped horns grew from the top of its dome, and ragged black wings sprouted from its back. It held a scythe in its hands — a weapon with a long handle and a curved blade at the end.

Runo screamed as the beast charged toward her.

CHAPTER 8

DRAGO SPEAKS

Over in Dan's school, his classmates gathered around him. Dan planted his foot on the desk in front of him, holding Drago's ball in his hand. He felt like a celebrity. "Hey, let me see that!" said a short boy with black hair.

"That is *sooo* cool! Is that the Bakugan I've been reading about on the web?" asked a blue-haired boy.

Dan proudly held up Drago's ball. "*Ta-daaaa!* Feast your eyes on the one and only Drago!"

"Is that the one that talks?" asked the first boy.

"Hey, Dan, make it say something," said the blue-haired boy.

A girl with ponytails looked thrilled. "Oh, I am so jealous! Mine hasn't said one word yet!"

The blue-haired boy sidled up to Dan. "Or maybe you just made the whole thing up, Danny!"

"I'll prove it to you, all right?" Dan said.

His classmates buzzed with excitement.

"Yeah, show us, Dan!"

"Make him talk!"

"Do it!"

"All right, all right already," Dan said. He looked at the ball in his hand. "Ready, Drago. It's showtime . . . Bakugan Stand!"

Nothing happened.

"Maybe it's busted," suggested the blue-haired student.

Panicked, Dan turned away from his classmates. He whispered to the Bakugan ball. "C'mon, Drago, say something! Bakugan Stand!"

Nothing happened. Dan tried again — and again.

"Bakugan Stand! Stand! Stand! Stand! STAND!"

But the Bakugan ball did not transform. Dan's classmates slowly backed away.

"You're embarrassing me, Drago," Dan whispered.

"Hey, Dan, forget Drago," the blue-haired boy said. "I'm wondering if you remembered to do your homework?"

"Yeah, 'cause if you didn't, Miss Purdy will be all over you!" the shorter boy pointed out.

"Oh no!" Dan wailed. "I forgot! I'm so done for!"

He put Drago's ball on his desk and started to plead with his fellow students. "Ya gotta help me or it's detention for life! Would you let me copy your notes? Please? You gotta help me out here, guys! Pleeeeeease!"

A small laugh came from Drago's ball, but Dan couldn't hear it.

What a pathetic human, Drago thought. *If he thinks I'm here for his personal amusement, he is sadly mistaken. I have a more important mission. To stop Vestroia's destruction!*

Drago strained to break out of the Bakugan ball. *Too much resistance . . . must summon strength!*

Drago pushed with all of his might, and the ball slowly rolled across the desktop.

Just then, Miss Purdy opened the door. The teacher had black hair pulled into a tight bun and wore glasses over her pinched face.

"Students, did you not hear the bell?" she scolded.

Everyone screamed and scrambled to get to their seats. One of the students tripped, knocking into Dan's desk. Drago's ball rolled off and fell to the floor!

Must resist being crushed!

The ball got kicked between the students' running feet, zooming around the room like a ball in a pinball machine. Then Dan spotted it.

"Drago!"

He ran after the ball. "Drago, stop! You've got to stop!"

"I'm trying!" Drago called out, but no one heard him over the panicked wails of the students. "Hurry! Catch me! I'm going to be sick!"

Drago's ball finally stopped rolling. It landed right at Miss Purdy's feet! The teacher picked it up.

"Who is responsible for bringing marbles into my classroom?" she asked. She looked up and saw Dan's panicked face. "Daniel! I'll see you after class."

"Yes, ma'am!" Daniel said quickly. He took the ball back from Miss Purdy and ran back to his seat.

How did I get myself into this predicament? Drago wondered.

Things calmed down a bit after that. Dan put Drago's ball inside his desk, and Miss Purdy began a math lesson. Drago contemplated his situation as the teacher droned on.

Somehow I must discern a way to move freely in this realm. But I must hurry because Vestroia is in danger. Naga is behind its destruction and I must stop him! But first, I must find him. . . .

Bored, Daniel propped his math book in front of him to shield himself from Miss Purdy's watchful eye. He took Drago's ball out of the desk. Then he started to scrub the ball with a toothbrush.

"Ah man, all that rollin' around on the floor sure messed you up, little guy," Dan said. "Now you're starting to look like new again. I bet you're wishing I'd do this all day and if you'd just talk to me, maybe I might."

Drago couldn't take it anymore. "Cease your scrubbing, human! I'm not your toy!" Drago yelled.

Dan was shocked. "Whoa, you scared me!" he cried out in surprise. He stood up. "Listen up, guys, he can talk. My Drago just talked to me, did you hear?"

Miss Purdy glared at him from the front of the room. "Daniel, that is quite enough!" she said. "Can you hear *my* voice? Can you, young man?"

"Yes, Miss Purdy," Daniel replied.

"Then I want you to listen very carefully to me," Miss Purdy said. "DETENTION FOR THE REST OF THE SEMESTER!"

"Noooo!" Dan wailed.

Later that day, Dan sat at his computer desk and glared down at Drago's Bakugan ball.

"All you had to do was talk," Dan complained. "Ah man, I wonder if all the other Brawlers out there have such stubborn Bakugan!"

He switched on his computer. "Okay, we're logged on." His friends' screens started to pop up. "Hey guys, how's it going?"

Runo's angry face took up all of Dan's screen. "Finally!" she yelled.

Startled, Dan fell back on his chair and landed on the floor. "Ow!"

"I hope you realize that it's all your fault I lost a Bakugan Brawl today!" Runo shrieked.

"Hey, Runo, give me a break, would ya?" Dan said, climbing back into his seat. "What are ya talking about?"

"That creep Masquerade came along and totally clobbered me," Runo said, a little more calmly.

Runo's screen got smaller, and Dan's other friends appeared.

"He's been winning battles all over the world," Marucho explained.

"Not to mention every chat room I checked is full of kids talking about Masquerade," Alice added.

"So what's his deal?" Dan asked.

Julie spoke up. "He's won every single battle he's been in and kids everywhere are losing their Bakugan like crazy! This is serious!"

"So Runo, did he get yours?" Dan asked.

Runo frowned. "Yeah. My precious Terrorclaw is gone for good."

Marucho looked worried. "We have to do something, Dan."

"Don't worry, guys, you can count on me," Dan said confidently. "If that dude comes anywhere near me looking for a battle, I'll win everyone's Bakugan back! Including your Terrorclaw, Runo. That masked guy's going down!"

"Awesome!" Runo said.

Dan stood up. "I don't care how good this Masquerade dude is, I'm gonna put my own Bakugan on the line and show him!"

Dan's friends gasped. Would he really do that for them?

"But what if you lose too?" Julie asked, worried.

"But I — I won't," Dan stammered. He actually hadn't thought about that.

"Do you know what he's ranked?" Runo asked.

Marucho knew, of course. "The last update on the web puts him bang on at number one."

"You have got to be kidding!" Dan replied, shocked. "That's impossible! The best Bakugan Brawler in the world should be Shun. Something's weird here. I have got to fix it!"

Dan pumped his fists in the air. "No matter the danger, no matter the risk, no matter the enemy, I will march to battle with my head held high and return victorious! This is my quest, to follow that star —"

Alice interrupted him. "Uh, Dan?"

"Now what!" Dan yelled. He felt pumped up from his rant.

"One question. How are you going to challenge Masquerade if you don't even know where he is?" Alice asked.

"Right," Dan said sheepishly. "Yeah, well, that's a good question."

Dan said good-bye to his friends. A few minutes later, he looked into the webcam. He had to issue a challenge. He just hoped Masquerade would accept it.

Dan smiled weirdly into the camera. "Hey Masquerade, Danno here. How's about a battle?"

Dan shook his head. "Oh man, that bites! How about this: Hey Masquerade, I'm sick and tired of you bullying Brawlers, so you're going down! That is, if you're brave enough to accept my challenge. Well, are you? Or are you going to keep hiding behind that creepy little mask of yours? Your Bakugan are mine, ya understand me! The name's Dan and I challenge you to a battle. I'm the new number one in town!"

Drago opened up and revealed his Dragonoid form.

"You're kidding," he said to Dan.

"Quiet, can't you see I'm just bluffing, Drago?" Dan asked. "Ya gotta trick him to come out and play — whoa! Did you just talk?"

"Listen to me, human," Drago said calmly. "I am not a toy. In your realm you see me only as a token trinket to battle for your pleasure. I ask you, is this just a game to you?"

"Hello!" Dan answered, waving his arms. "This is the greatest game ever! I love everything about Bakugan! It makes me feel alive, in control, and the best part is, I love winning!"

Drago was silent.

"What's wrong, Drago? Are you saying you don't like to battle?" Dan asked. "I thought that's what you were programmed for. I'm not gettin' this."

Drago stubbornly closed his ball. "Bakugan is *more* than a game."

Dan didn't understand Drago at all. He just knew this Masquerade guy was out of control, and somebody had to stop him. He turned back to the camera.

"Hey, Masquerade, I know you're out there, so if you're listening, what do you say you show yourself and we have a battle? Winner takes all. Loser walks away with nothing.

"But I warn you I'm good," Dan continued. "And my Dragonoid and I are gonna blow your doors off. Nobody bullies the Brawlers and gets away with it! So here's the deal, pal. Tomorrow after school, underneath the railroad bridge at Palmdale Avenue — that's where it's going down! And you better show up! Do I make myself clear, Masquerade?"

Dan shut down his computer. He had issued his challenge.

He just hoped Masquerade would take it!

CHAPTER 10

DRAGO REBELS

"C'mon, c'mon, out of the way! Move it!"

Dan raced through the streets of the city, pushing people out of his way.

"This is gonna be sweet. I am so pumped, he won't stand a chance," Dan said as he ran. "Let's go! He just better show up."

Dan turned a corner and saw the bridge above him, just ahead. A figure stood under the bridge, waiting for him.

Dan skidded to a stop. "You're here!"

But it wasn't Masquerade.

Shuji turned to face Dan, an evil grin on his face. Akira popped out from behind him.

"We've been waitin' for ya," Akira said.

"Too bad your buddy Masquerade didn't show up," Shuji taunted.

Dan was furious. "Not you two again!" he yelled. "I do not have time for this! Beat it!"

But Shuji didn't budge. "You owe me!" he replied angrily. "I demand a rematch. So pull out your cards and let's get this battle underway."

Shuji whipped out a Gate Card and held it up. "Ready or not!"

Dan sighed. "Give me a break. This is a complete waste of my time," he said. "Well, might as well get this over with."

He took a Gate Card out of his pocket. "You want a piece of me, then you got it!"

"Yeah!" Shuji cheered.

The boys threw out their cards. "Bakugan Field Open!"

The battle started pretty much the way Dan expected. Shuji hadn't become a master Brawler overnight. Dan quickly took down his Robotallian and Gargonoid.

Soon he was poised to win the whole thing. His Pyrus Serpenoid was standing on the field. Dan knew Shuji had only one Bakugan left — his Ventus Falconeer.

"Ready to lose your Ventus?" Dan asked.

"Bring it!" Shuji shouted.

Dan held up Drago's ball and whispered to it. "Okay, Drago, finish this for me."

He rolled the ball onto the field. "Bakugan Brawl!"

The ball landed right behind Serpenoid. "Bakugan Stand!"

Red light flashed across the field, and Drago transformed into his true form. The winged Dragonoid towered over Serpenoid, flapping his wings.

Shuji's eyes were as wide as pizzas. "A-a Dragonoid!"

Drago felt free for the first time in a long time. *When he releases me, I can move around freely in this world*, he realized.

Dan felt great. He was about to take care of Shuji once and for all.

"Here it comes, Drago. Ability Activate Now!" Dan yelled.

Dan threw out the card, and a blazing wall of fire formed around Drago's body.

"But my Fire Wall won't be effective against a beast with wind attributes," Drago said. Instead of moving forward to attack, he stayed right where he was.

"Drago, what are you doing! We're right in the middle of a battle!" Dan yelled.

"I do not take orders, human!" Drago replied firmly.

Dan couldn't believe it. "What? Get in there!"

Shuji watched them argue and grinned. "This is the opening I've been waiting for." He threw a new ball onto the field. "Bakugan Brawl!"

The green ball landed in front of Serpenoid. "Bakugan Stand!"

The ball opened and transformed into a Ventus

Falconeer. The green beast had the head of an eagle, a human-like body, and large wings.

"Falconeer Power Level 300 Gs," the Baku-pod reported.

Dan wasn't sweating. He knew Drago had 340 Gs.

"Hey, I might be low on power, but your Dragonoid is useless against my Falconeer's Wind Attribute," Shuji pointed out. "And just to be safe, I'm gonna amp it up a notch!"

Shuji held up a card. "Ability Activate Jump Over! And correlation between Ventus and Pyrus!"

A swirling funnel of wind surrounded Falconeer. He flew up high over Drago's Fire Wall and hovered there, flapping his wings.

"He jumped right over the Fire Wall!" Dan cried.

"One way to fight fire is to use a little wind," Shuji said confidently. "You thought your Dragonoid had more power than my Falconeer. Wrong! Fire is trumped by Wind."

"Falconeer Power 400 Gs," the Baku-pod reported.

"What do we do, Drago?" Dan called out.

Falconeer dove down and latched onto Drago's neck with his sharp claws. Drago tried to throw him off.

"Falconeer! Our fight is not with each other!" Drago said.

"I battle by using my instinct, Dragonoid," Falconeer hissed. Then he bit into Drago's neck.

Drago roared and reared back, sending Falconeer flying. The Ventus beast landed on his feet in front of Drago.

"Come to your senses," Drago pleaded. "It is negative energy that drives you!"

Falconeer jumped up and plunged his beak into Drago's neck again.

"Drago!" Dan cried.

Drago summoned his strength. "You leave me no choice!"

He used all of his energy to draw the Fire Wall close in around the two of them. The suffocating heat from the flames snuffed out the wind tunnel around Falconeer. The beast turned back into a Bakugan ball and returned to Shuji.

"The Fire Wall smothered the wind!" Dan realized.

Shuji stared at Dan, his mouth open. The Bakugan field disappeared around them.

"You lose!" Dan cheered.

"Why do you keep doing this to me!" Shuji wailed.

Akira frowned at his big brother. "Ah man, didn't I tell you not to use Falconeer? But no, mister big shot here wouldn't listen. And now look what happened!"

Shuji ran past Akira through an opening in the chain link fence. "Can it, Akira! I'm going home to mommy!"

"Hey!" Akira called after his brother. He turned back to Dan. "Catch ya later, Slick!"

Dan laughed. "If you wanna lose, you guys just give me a call!" he yelled after them.

Dan looked down at Drago's ball. "Hey, Drago, way to pull off the win. To be honest, I was gettin' a bit nervous back there."

Drago didn't say anything.

"Oh, the silent treatment again," Dan said. "Well this time I'm not fallin' for it. You can . . ."

Dan paused as he heard a new sound — the sound of footsteps behind him.

Dan turned. The sound was coming from a dark chamber cut into the concrete base of the bridge. Then a voice came out of the darkness.

"I'm looking for Dan Kuso."

CHAPTER 11

SO LONG, SERPENOID!

That you, Masquerade?" Dan called out.

Masquerade stepped out of the darkness. Dan checked out his opponent: long white coat, purple pants, a wavy mess of yellow hair. The strangest thing was the blue mask that covered his eyes and extended down his cheeks, leaving only his mouth and nose visible.

"So you decided to show up, and I get to put a face to the name," Dan said. "Well, Masquerade, I heard you've been stealing my buddy's Bakugan. How come?"

"Ha!" Masquerade replied.

"We put a lot of time into organizing this game, and there's no way I'm gonna let you or anyone mess it up!" Dan said, feeling tough. "It stops here, Masquerade!"

"It's time to Battle, Dan," Masquerade said calmly. He held up a Gate Card. "Ready?"

Dan held up his first card too. "Field Open!"

Both boys threw down their Gate Cards. They joined end to end to form the battlefield between them.

"Gate Card . . . Set!" both boys yelled.

Now concentrate, Dan told himself. He couldn't lose this one.

Masquerade held up another card. He threw it onto the field, and it vanished into the white light surrounding the Gate Cards.

"Your move," Masquerade said.

I wonder what he threw down? Dan thought. *Guess I'll use my Serpenoid. It'll get a nice G power boost from my Gate Card.*

Dan threw out the Bakugan ball. It landed exactly where he wanted it.

"Come on, Serpenoid, do some damage!" Dan yelled. "Bakugan Stand!"

Serpenoid broke free from its ball, uncoiling its red and orange body. It hissed at Masquerade.

"Ability Activate. Reaper Stand!" Masquerade cried out, as he threw his Bakugan.

Dan gasped as Reaper appeared on the field. The horned, winged Darkus beast looked positively evil.

"Reaper Power Level 370 Gs," said the Baku-pod. "Serpenoid Power Level 320 Gs."

"Gate Card Open now!" Dan commanded.

The card flipped over, giving Serpenoid a huge boost

of G power. Giant flames rose up against the Pyrus beast, heating up the field.

"Serpenoid Power Level increase to 620 Gs," the Baku-pod reported.

Dan was feeling pretty confident. "Okay, Masquerade, time to put up or shut up. Let's see you trump that!"

Masquerade held up a card. "Ability Activate . . . Dimension Four!"

He waved the card over his head. In an instant, the fiery flames surrounding Serpenoid vanished. The field was calm once again.

"What's that?" Dan asked.

"Just one of my pets," Masquerade said calmly. "It's an Ability Card called Dimension Four."

"Serpenoid Power drop to 320 Gs," the Baku-pod announced.

Masquerade laughed smugly as his Reaper charged across the field, lifting his scythe over his head. He slashed a hole into the battle space above Serpenoid.

"No! Serpenoid!" Dan screamed.

He watched in horror as the hole sucked Serpenoid inside. His Pyrus beast was gone!

"Oh no!" Dan cried. "He took my beast right out of the battle!"

CHAPTER 12

FEAR THE REAPER

What incredible power! Drago realized.

Reaper turned back into a Bakugan ball and bounced into Masquerade's hand.

The first round was over, but Dan still had two chances to catch up. He held up a new Bakugan ball.

"Bakugan Brawl!" he cried.

The ball landed on a Gate Card on the field.

"Bakugan Stand!"

Dan's ball transformed into his Pyrus Saurus. Masquerade countered by throwing out his Reaper again.

Dan knew his Saurus couldn't beat Reaper head to head. But he had a strategy.

"Ability Activate! Saurus Glow!" he yelled, throwing down a card.

A circle of flames rose up, surrounding Saurus. Rings of fiery red heat pulsated around him, and Saurus's normally red body turned white from the heat.

"You beat my Gate Card, but you won't be able to override the power of my Ability Card!" Dan said confidently.

But Masquerade didn't look worried at all. He waved another card over his head.

"Double Dimension, Activate."

The power of Masquerade's card cancelled out Dan's Ability Card. Once again, the flames died out around Saurus. His extra power boost was gone.

"Ah man, he shut down the power of my Ability!" Dan complained.

Reaper charged across the field, slamming into Saurus. The purple light above the field ripped open, sucking Saurus inside.

"No fair! I want my Bakugan back!" Dan cried.

"Sorry, but no can do," Masquerade said. "Once the Doom Card is played, the battle is over."

"Doom Card?" Dan asked. He suddenly remembered the strange card Masquerade had thrown at the start of the battle. This didn't sound good.

"Yes, Dan, the Doom Card," Masquerade replied. "Once you throw it down, it overpowers all cards, sending the defeated Bakugan into another dimension for eternity."

"You're kidding!" Dan said.

Drago was shocked. "The Doom Dimension!" he

said. "He's right, human. A Bakugan can never return from the Doom Dimension. There we meet our eternal demise. Nothing is feared more!"

Dan faced Masquerade, angry. "Now I know why you're stealing everyone's Bakugan. But the question is, why are you wrecking our game?"

"Dan, Dan, Dan," Masquerade said. "Whoever said this was just a game? Every single battle is real."

Every battle is real. Drago had said exactly the same thing!

Dan felt a surge of energy pump through his body. He couldn't lose. Not now!

"Gate Card Set!" he yelled, throwing a new card out onto the field. Then he looked down at the last Bakugan ball in his hand. "C'mon, Drago, this is our one shot at it."

Dan and Masquerade hurled their Bakugan balls onto the field. They landed facing each other and then transformed into Reaper and Drago. The Dragonoid opened his jaws wide and lunged at Reaper. But the Darkus beast stopped him with the handle of his scythe. Drago chomped down on the metal bar.

"Why are you doing this?" Drago asked Reaper. "Do you realize what's happening in Vestroia?"

"This does not concern me," Reaper answered.

"Of course it does!" Drago said.

Reaper pushed Drago back and began to slash at the Dragonoid with his blade. Drago dodged each blow, lunging at Reaper with his clawed feet.

"I am a soldier of this dimension and I am free to team up with a human," Reaper said. "Then I can inherit infinite power."

"You fool!" Drago said angrily.

Reaper flapped his ragged wings and flew high above Drago's head. "I've had enough of you. It's time to send you to the Doom Dimension, Dragonoid!"

"Come on, Drago!" Dan yelled.

Reaper lowered his scythe, slicing into the purple light surrounding the field.

"Have a pleasant journey!" he said, laughing darkly.

But no portal to the Doom Dimension appeared. Drago pushed back hard against Reaper, flapping his wings.

Masquerade was shocked. "What!?"

CHAPTER 13

THE ULTIMATE CHALLENGE

Drago wasn't down yet. Dan still had more moves to make.

"Drago! Gate Card Open! Activate Fire Storm!" Dan yelled.

The Gate Card flipped over, and a sea of flames sprang up from the battle field. Drago's body began to glow with the heat. But Reaper kept pushing against Drago, trying to force him into the Doom Dimension.

Dan held up a card. "We're down to our last card. This is it . . ."

Dan stopped. Drago was roaring in pain. The extra firepower seemed to be consuming Drago, instead of making him more powerful.

"What's wrong?" Dan called out.

"Ultimate Boost!" Drago cried out, his voice filled with pain.

Dan gasped as the card in his hand shattered into pieces. Above him, Drago began to glow white with the intense heat. The fiery flames licked across the field, out of control.

BOOM!

The field exploded in a blast of light and heat.

"Drago, Drago, where are you!" Dan screamed.

The Bakugan field dissolved, and everything was normal again. Dan looked down to see Drago's Bakugan ball at his feet. He knelt down and picked it up, sighing with relief.

"I spared him for you," Masquerade said.

Dan wasn't sure what to think. What was up with this guy?

"You realize I could have captured your Bakugan but I decided against it," Masquerade continued. "It's been a slice, Dan. Later."

Masquerade turned to leave.

"Wait! I can beat you! I know I can!" Dan yelled.

Masquerade stopped. "Bakugan is not a mere game, kiddo." He laughed. "There are other dimensions and powers involved, Dan. It's a battle that can lead to the destruction of the entire world."

"For real?" Dan asked.

Masquerade nodded. "And the only way to stop it is for you to defeat me."

"This is crazy!" Dan cried.

Masquerade just laughed and walked away. He looked down at Reaper's Bakugan ball in his hand.

"So, human, that was a Dragonoid?" Reaper asked. "I wonder if he fought at full power?"

"No clue. And unfortunately he didn't possess what I am searching for," Masquerade answered. "But I will remember Dan Kuso and his Bakugan, Drago."

Dan jumped to his feet as he watched them walk away.

He had promised his friends he would beat Masquerade. But he had lost. He didn't get their Bakugan back. And two of his best beasts were lost to the Doom Dimension forever!

Dan shook his fist in the air. "I will beat you, Masquerade!"

DAN KUSO

12-year-old Dan helped to create the Bakugan game when the cards first fell from the sky. His goal is to be the number one Brawler in the world, and he likes to use Pyrus Bakugan with fire attributes to heat up a Brawl. Like his Bakugan, Dan has a fiery temper sometimes, and he loves to trash talk his opponents. He battles with a Pyrus Dragonoid named Drago.

DRAGO /////////////////////////////////

A DRAGONOID WITH A PYRUS ATTRIBUTE,
DRAGO IS FROM A PARALLEL DIMENSION
CALLED VESTROIA. HE BECAME TRAPPED
ON EARTH AFTER A HOLE WAS RIPPED BETWEEN
THE TWO DIMENSIONS. NOW HE IS DAN'S BAKU-
GAN, BUT HE REFUSES TO TAKE ORDERS FROM
HUMANS AND SOMETIMES GIVES DAN A HARD
TIME IN BATTLE. DAN DOESN'T MIND SO MUCH,
BECAUSE DRAGO'S AMAZING POWER MAKES UP
FOR HIS ATTITUDE!

RUNO MISAKI

Tomboy Runo isn't afraid to battle even the toughest Brawlers. She's got a lot of energy, but her battling style can sometimes be uneven. She likes to blow away her opponents with her Ventus Bakugan, Tigrerra.

TIGRERRA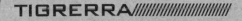

Runo's Bakugan beast looks like a tiger. It is a Ventus Bakugan, which means it has wind attributes. These Bakugan are as fast and powerful as hurricane winds.

MARUCHO VIGARO

Marucho is 11 years old, but he's smarter than people twice his age. His sharp mind is a storehouse for every Bakugan fact, and he uses that data to develop battle strategies. That sometimes backfires on Marucho, who needs to learn that sometimes you need to trust your instincts over facts. He likes to use Aquos Bakugan in battle but he is also a master of combination play, bringing more than one type of Bakugan to a Brawl.

PREYAS //////////////////////////////

Marucho's Bakugan has an unusual power—it is an Aquos Bakugan, but can change its attribute in battle. That works well for Marucho, who is good at combining attributes in a Brawl.

JULIE MAKIMOTO

Some people might call bubbly Julie an "airhead," but her easy-going manner is deceiving. When Julie battles, she uses down-to-earth Sub Terra Bakugan. Her direct battling style helps her pummel her opponents.

GOREM///////////////////////////////

Julie's Sub Terra Bakugan is as tough as he looks. He's got an extremely heavy body. When Gorem gets angry, only Julie can calm him down.

SHUN KAZAMI

Shun helped Dan create the rules of Bakugan, but the two Brawlers are as different as night and day. Dan is loud, and Shun is quiet. Dan has lots of friends, and Shun is a loner. Dan can't break the top ten in the rankings, and Shun is almost always number one. Shun prefers to use Ventrus wind attributes in battle.

SKYRESS //////////////////////////

Shun's guardian beast is a Ventus Bakugan from the Skyress class. The tips of her long tails are as sharp as knives, but that's not her only power. She can see through objects. And most impressive, Skyress can resurrect if she's been taken down on the field.

ALICE GEHABICH

14-year-old Alice is thoughtful and sweet. She likes to give advice to the other Brawlers, and thinks of Marucho as a little brother. The other Brawlers don't know much about Alice. Is it possible she's hiding some kind of secret from them?

SHUJI

This big Brawler loves to bully people into battling
with him—especially Dan. Shuji may look tough, but
he doesn't have the skills to back up his boasting. But
he'll keep trying to beat Dan no matter how many
times he loses.

MASQUERADE

This mysterious Brawler appeared out of nowhere and starting beating Bakugan Brawlers everywhere. Thanks to his Doom Dimension card, his opponents' Bakugan are lost forever. Masquerade brawls with his Darkus Bakugan, a perfect fit for his dark personality.

HYDRANOID///////////////

Besides Reaper, Masquerade also uses Hydranoid, a Darkus beast from the Draganoid class. This combination results in a cruel and unforgiving beast. Hydranoid may move slowly in battle, but its power is hard to beat.

REAPER

This Darkus beast is from the Reaper class, a type of Bakugan known for battling with intense fury. Masquerade's Reaper wields a weapon with a curved blade called a scythe. When Masquerade uses the Doom Dimension card, Reaper uses the scythe to send Bakugan into eternal darkness.

HOW DO YOU ROLL?™

ROLL WITH THE SKILL OF A MASTER BRAWLER AND ACHIEVE TRUE BATTLE GLORY!
GRAB YOUR FAVORITE BAKUGAN™ AND UNLEASH YOUR INNER WARRIOR AS YOU
WATCH YOUR BAKUGAN™ TRANSFORM INTO AWESOME, POWERFUL BEASTS!
THE TIME FOR BATTLE IS NOW, ONLY YOU CAN DECIDE THE FATE OF THE GALAXY!

VISIT **BAKUGAN.COM** TO LEARN MORE ABOUT BAKUGAN™ BATTLE BRAWLERS.™